Copyright © 2005 by NordSüd Verlag AG, Gossau Zürich, Switzerland
First published in Switzerland under the title *Kunos große Fahrt*.
English translation copyright © 2005 by North-South Books Inc., New York

First published in the United States, Great Britain, Canada, Australia,
and New Zealand in 2005 by North-South Books, an imprint of
NordSüd Verlag AG, Gossau Zürich, Switzerland.

Distributed in the United States by North-South Books Inc., New York.
Library of Congress Cataloging-in-Publication Data is available.
A CIP catalogue record for this book is available from The British Library.
ISBN 0-7358-2027-9 (trade edition) 10 9 8 7 6 5 4 3 2 1
ISBN 0-7358-2028-7 (library edition) 10 9 8 7 6 5 4 3 2 1

Printed in Italy

Ken's Great Adventure

By Klaus Merz

Illustrated by Hannes Binder

Translated by Marianne Martens

North-South Books

New York / London

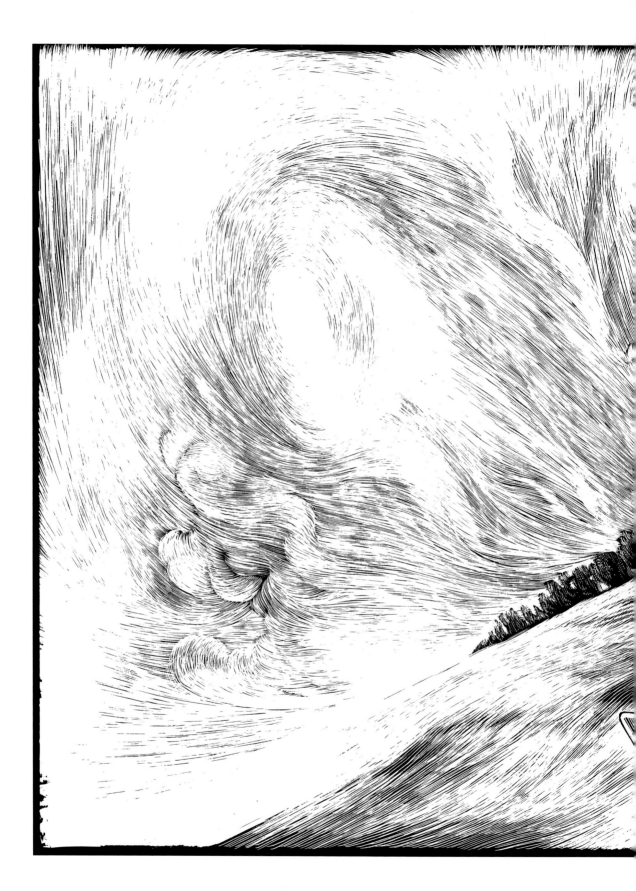

At first, all that could be heard was a quiet buzzing in the air. And then he appeared. Bright eyes peered out from under the blue of the ocean steadily taking in the asphalt before him.

Over his left temple sat the continent of North America. The right side of his head was protected by Asia. Africa covered the back.

At home, with his father's light-up globe before him, he'd painted the
world onto his helmet—latitudes and longitudes in grey; large bodies
of water in blue; green and brown, the ground he would travel—first

with his finger, then later on his scooter. His sister had given him the helmet. She no longer needed it since she'd traded her moped for a racing bike.

Ken journeyed on back roads across the countryside.
The boy with the huge helmet on his head brought to mind Atlas,
the giant on whose shoulders the heavens rested according to Greek
mythology.

He pushed off with his right foot and glided on his silver scooter across the world.

Beyond the forest, he stopped, took off his helmet, and ran his fingers through his flattened hair. He held the helmet in front of his chest, studied the route, and nodded.

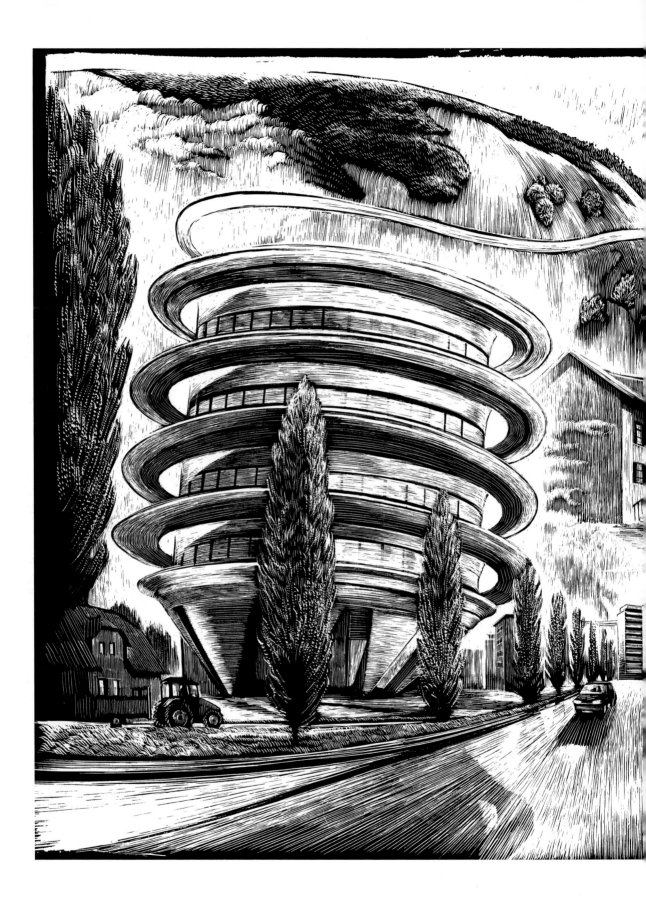

Ken's path kept the lake and the villages on the right, as he
headed north, toward the pole.

He was off to experience the world. He knew that he just needed
to go toward the North Pole and continue straight ahead all the way
around, in order to return home again.

Up in the hills it started to grow dark.
A truck forced Ken onto the side of the road. Hungry and thirsty, he
pushed a chocolate bar through the open visor, followed with some
water, and attached his flashlight to the handlebars.

A warning sign on the back of a truck reminded him that an elk could cross his path at any point. "Don't be afraid, Ken," he told himself. He switched feet on the scooter and continued on his journey.

The moon rose and brightened the night, throwing Ken's shadow on the asphalt. He crossed broad landscapes, glided through villages, and past a suburb to a city.

To keep from giving in to exhaustion, he refused to look into the warmly lit houses and apartment buildings. He kept his eyes on his shadow, and on the edge of the road.

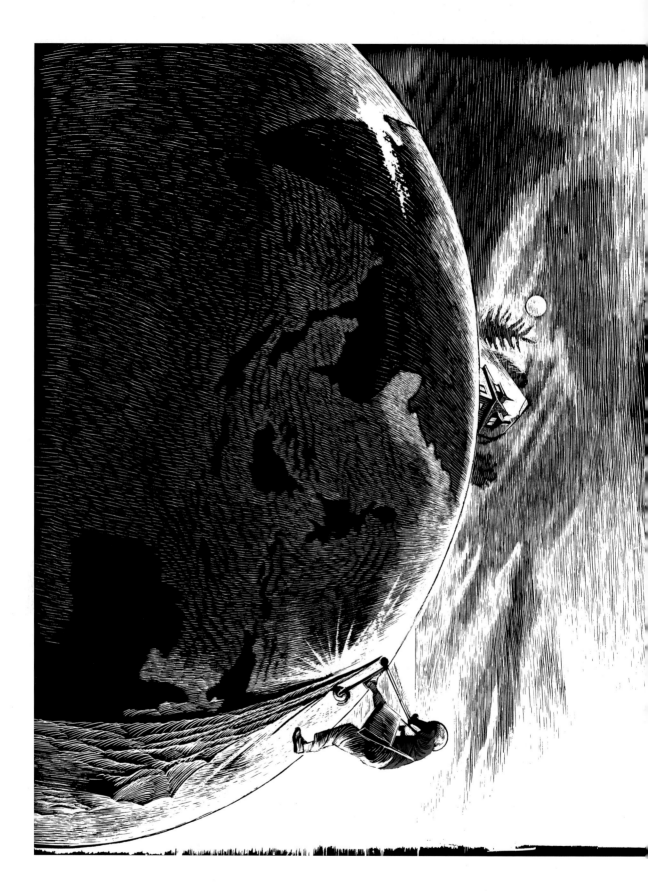

Until finally, long after dark, he started climbing back up from the
bottom half of the world, back toward his own home. From way down
the road, he could hear his family calling for him, waiting and worried:
"Ken, come home! Come home, Ken!"

Ken's heart pounded. He was dead tired. But he was not afraid. Because that morning, before his great adventure, he had decided that from then on, he could handle the world on his own.